The
Return
of Johnny
Kemp

The Return of Johnny Kemp

Keith Gray

Barrington Stoke

First published in 2009 in Great Britain by
Barrington Stoke Ltd
18 Walker Street, Edinburgh, EH3 7LP

www.barringtonstoke.co.uk

This edition first published 2014

A CIP catalogue record for this book is available
from the British Library upon request

ISBN: 978-1-78112-421-5

Printed in China by Leo

Contents

CHAPTER 1

Me

It was 5 to 8 on Monday morning. They were already waiting for me.

My mobile rang. I heard its heavy metal ring tone, but couldn't see it. I was packing my school bag and my room was a mess. It was always a mess. My P.E. kit was stuffed under my bed. My Maths book was at the bottom of a pile of magazines. I didn't have a clue where I'd left my R.E. homework. I panicked for a second when I couldn't find my keys. But then I found them in my school bag. My phone rang again. I found it in my coat pocket – and my coat was on the floor.

I looked at the phone. It was my friend Gary ringing me. I answered his call. "Yeah. What's up?" I said.

Gary came round to my house every day on the way to school. Maybe he was running late today? His voice sounded weird. "Dan? Dan? Is that you?" he asked.

"Who else would it be?" I asked.

Gary was panting. He sounded like he'd been running. "Dan, have you looked outside?"

I hadn't bothered to open my bedroom curtains yet. "Why?" I asked. "What's happening? Has it snowed again?" It had been a brilliant weekend of snowball fights.

"Go and look!" Gary said. His breath was loud and heavy over the phone.

I kept my mobile by my ear with one hand and pulled open the curtains with my other hand. My bedroom window looked out over the back garden and into the alley at the back of our house. It was a bright February morning. There hadn't been any fresh snow overnight. It was just 2-day-old grey slush everywhere.

"And?" I asked. "What am I supposed to be looking at?"

"Can't you see them?"

I pulled my curtains as far back as they would go. I looked up and down the row of back gardens and along the alley in both directions. "See who?" I asked.

"The Baxter brothers," Gary said. He wasn't panting because he was out of breath – he was scared. "They're right outside your house."

I felt my stomach go as cold as the dirty snow.

I ran to my mum's bedroom at the front of the house. She was having breakfast downstairs. She hadn't opened her curtains yet either. Her bed wasn't made and her alarm clock was on the floor on the far side of the room. She must have thrown it there, angry at it for waking her up.

I didn't yank her curtains open like I'd done mine. Instead I peered around the edge of them just enough to see down to the street outside. And stood up against our garden wall were Neil and Matty Baxter. Neil had a hoodie on. Matty's cap was pulled low over his eyes.

I swore loudly.

"That's what I thought," Gary said. "And you know why they're there, don't you? You know why they're waiting for you."

I was gripping the phone hard. "Johnny Kemp. He's coming back to school today," I said.

"Yeah, and that means you're dead," Gary said. "You know that, don't you? He said he was going to kill you. He told everyone."

"I know," I said.

"He reckoned the first day he came back he was going to stomp you into the ground," Gary said.

"Yeah, Gary. I know."

"He said he was going to smash your head in two, Dan," Gary went on. "I mean, he's really, really, really going to kill you."

"Yeah, OK, Gary. OK. I know!" I was scared too now.

Just over two weeks ago, Johnny Kemp had been excluded from our school. He was a bully and a thug. He was mean like barbed wire, dangerous like broken glass. Everyone was scared of him. I think the teachers had been looking for just one more bad thing, one more reason, so that they could exclude him. I was the person who'd given them that reason. I was the one who'd got Johnny Kemp kicked out of school. That's why he wanted to get me back.

I looked down at the Baxter brothers waiting on the street outside. They were Johnny Kemp's best friends. I went as close to the window as I dared and peered both ways along our street. There was an old man walking his dog. There was a woman scraping the ice off her car's windscreen. I couldn't see Kemp anywhere. Was he hidden behind one of the parked cars? Or was he waiting out of sight around the corner?

I reckoned Neil and Matty Baxter were there to grab me and drag me to where Kemp was waiting. He was waiting somewhere he could kick me in without anyone seeing. Somewhere he could take all the time he needed.

"Where are you?" I asked Gary.

"At the bus stop on the corner," he said. "I saw the Baxter brothers, but no way did I want them to see me."

"Is Kemp there too?" I wanted to know.

"I can't see him," Gary said. "But I bet he's somewhere near by."

I gripped the phone. I gritted my teeth.

I walked up and down my mum's room.

"Dan?" Gary asked. "Dan? You still there? What're you going to do?"

"I don't know what I can do," I said.

"If I was you," Gary told me, "I'd start saying I was ill. I'd tell my mum I had smallpox or scarlet fever or something. Anything. Just so I didn't have to go to school today. If I was you, Dan, I'd make sure I stayed ill for a really, really long time. Being ill at home has got to be better than being dead at school."

CHAPTER 2
Mum

"Wait there," I told Gary. "I'll call you back!"

I ended the call and shoved my phone into my pocket. Then I went downstairs to the kitchen.

My mum was standing at the sink with her back to me as I came in the door. She was wearing her red dressing-gown that was easily as old as I was. Her curly blonde hair was here, there and everywhere. On the table behind her was a half-empty mug of coffee and a half-full ashtray. She turned when she heard me. She looked tired. But then she always looked tired.

"Mum," I said. "Mum, listen!" I was in a hurry to tell her that I had one hell of a problem waiting for me outside.

"I asked you to do these dishes last night," she said. She had the sleeves of her dressing-gown pushed up to her elbows and soap suds on her hands.

"Yeah, I know. I'm sorry," I said. "I was going to do them, but –"

"Always 'but' with you, isn't it, Dan? Always 'but'."

I felt bad then. I mumbled another "sorry". Mum worked in a posh hotel in town. It was so posh that just one room for one night cost more than Mum got paid for a whole week's work. She'd been on the late shift again last night and hadn't come home until midnight.

"Did you even bother to tidy your bedroom?" she asked.

I looked at my feet. I didn't answer.

She dried her hands on her dressing-gown. "Some help from you would be nice, Dan," she said. "Just a little bit now and again. We talked about this when your dad left. You said you understood."

I moved from one foot to the other. I hated it when she talked about Dad.

"Is your brother up yet?" Mum asked.

"Don't know," I said. "I think so."

"Well, could you make sure he is then, please?" Her voice was sharp. "We're all going to be late if we don't get a move on."

I could see she wasn't in a good mood this morning – not with me or anyone else. But it was now or never. I had to ask. "Mum?" I said. "Is it OK if I don't go to school today?"

She didn't answer. She turned her back to me and filled the kettle at the tap to make more coffee.

I watched her plug the kettle in, waiting for her to answer.

"Mum …?"

"Of course you've got to go to school," she said.

"But, Mum, listen …" I began.

The kettle made a grumbling noise as the water inside began to boil. When Mum turned to look at me she was angrier than ever.

I was quick to talk first, to try and explain. "Remember all that stuff with Johnny Kemp? Yeah? About him being excluded and that? Well, he's back at school today."

She shook her head. "I haven't got time for this!" The kettle began to hiss.

"But he said he's going to beat me up," I said.

Mum just scowled at the clock on the wall. "I've got to see someone at the bank later, so I'll need you to go to the supermarket for me. I'm just not going to get a chance. I'll write you a list of what we need."

I needed her to understand. "It's true, Mum. Honest. He said he would."

She gripped the handle of the kettle, ready to pick it up the instant it boiled. "I'll leave you enough money to get the bus, so you can go right after school."

"But that's what I'm saying, Mum. I can't go to school today."

Steam rose from the kettle.

"You're going to school today," Mum snapped. "I've got to go to work this morning even if I did do the late shift last night. I've got to go begging to the bank manager again. Believe you me – I really don't want to do that either. But I have to. We all have things we have to do, Daniel. And yours is having to go to school."

"But, Mum –" I said.

"Don't 'but' me!" she shouted. The kettle juddered as the hot water inside bubbled and steamed.

That was when my younger brother, Jason, walked into the kitchen. He was all snagged up in his school jumper. He had a broken arm, still in the plaster cast, and he couldn't pull his jumper over his head.

"What's all the shouting about?" he asked.

The kettle clicked off – the water had boiled at last. Mum looked about ready to bite my head off. But she took a deep breath and splashed the hot water into her mug. She said to me, "I haven't got time to walk Jason to school, so you'll have to do it for me."

She saw my mouth open, ready to argue.

"No 'buts'," she warned.

I began to wish I'd taken Gary's advice and pretended I had smallpox.

CHAPTER 3
Jason

"Why are we going this way?" Jason asked.

"Shut up and do as you're told!"

I hefted my school bag onto my shoulder. Then I dragged my brother by his good arm, the one that wasn't broken, out of the back door and into the garden.

Jason was eleven, three years younger than me and still in his first year at our school. He had a shocking frizz of red hair and it got him called names and picked on by a lot of the other kids. But he was tough. He never let it show how much the name-calling hurt him.

I dragged him all the way across the garden to the back gate that led onto the alley at the back of our house. It was cold. We were both wearing gloves and scarves. We could see our foggy breath. The wet, slushy snow was slippery under our feet.

"What's going on?" Jason asked.

"Shush," I told him. I opened our tall back gate and poked my head out into the alley. I looked both ways and I couldn't see Johnny Kemp or the Baxter brothers anywhere.

"What're you doing?" Jason asked.

"Shut up," I told him. I took my mobile out of my pocket and called Gary.

He answered on the second ring. "Are you OK?"

"Yeah, yeah," I said. "I'm fine. For now, anyway."

"Where are you?" he asked.

"I'm going out the back way, along the alley. No way am I going to risk the street if the Baxter brothers are there. Can you still see them?"

Gary didn't answer.

"Gary? Are the Baxter brothers still outside my house? Is Kemp there too?"

"I don't know," he said.

I didn't understand. "What do you mean, you don't know?" I asked.

"I didn't want to hang around," he said. "I was scared Kemp might see me or something."

I was shocked. "You didn't wait for me?"

"It's not my fault. I didn't think you were going to come to school today. I thought you were going to say you were ill," Gary said.

Now I was angry. "That's great! Thanks a lot, Gary. Great friend you are!"

He started trying to make some sort of excuse, but I couldn't be bothered to listen so I ended the call. I shoved the phone back in my pocket. What sort of a best friend was he? I couldn't believe Gary had run off and left me to face the Baxter brothers, and probably Johnny Kemp too, all by myself.

"Dan?" Jason asked. "What's going on?"

"Look, just shut up and listen, OK? If I tell you to run, then run, right? And I mean fast."

"Only if you tell me what's happening," he said.

"Johnny Kemp is what's happening. He's coming back to school today and he's going to be after me," I told him.

I opened the back gate again – just a little – and poked my head out into the alley. There was still no one to be seen.

I held onto my school bag in one hand and Jason in the other. "Come on," I said, and I dragged him through the gate.

We walked quickly along the alley. We splashed through slushy puddles. I kept checking back along the alley. I reckoned if we could make it to Murray Street at the end, then we could run as far as the playing fields. It was the longer way to school, but I hoped the Baxter brothers wouldn't work out that we'd gone that way. With any luck they might think I was still at home and end up waiting on the street all day.

"Hurry up," I said to Jason, pulling on his good arm.

"I'm coming, I'm coming," he said.

But that was when I saw Matty Baxter appear at the end of the alley. He stood with his hands in his pockets, shoulders hunched, cap pulled low over his eyes. He was blocking our way onto Murray Street.

"Back this way," I said to Jason. But when we turned around there was Neil Baxter blocking the other end of the alley.

I wanted to run back to our gate and into the safety of our garden, but I didn't think we'd be quick enough. Neil Baxter was closer – he'd get there first.

'Coming this way was a big mistake,' I thought. There were high fences and walls on both sides of us. It felt like a trap. Maybe the Baxter brothers guessed all along that I'd come this way.

"What do they want?" Jason asked.

I didn't answer him. I just swore under my breath. I knew they wanted me.

Matty Baxter started walking towards us. When I looked back the other way, Neil Baxter was coming too. They wanted to trap us between them. I grabbed Jason and lifted him up so he could get hold of the top of the nearest fence with his good hand.

"What're you doing? Get off!" Jason shouted. He tried to get away from me and climb down again.

The Baxter brothers saw what I was doing and started to run.

"Just get over," I hissed at Jason. I boosted him up as high as I could. "Go on!"

He scrambled over the fence into next-door's garden. I heard him drop down the other side.

The Baxter brothers were running fast, splashing through the snow and slush. I threw my school bag over the fence, then jumped up at the fence, grabbing the top. I kicked at it with my slippery shoes, trying to heave myself over. My shoes banged against the wood. With a grunt I got one leg across the top. And I tumbled down the other side and hit the wet ground hard.

It hurt, but I was quick to get back on my feet.

Jason just stood there. "What're we doing, Dan?" he asked.

"Trying not to get my face smashed in," I told him.

There was a shed near the back of the garden. I grabbed my bag and shoved Jason into the small gap between the shed and the side fence. Again he tried to squirm away from me, but I had him by the collar and forced him to crouch down. Luckily the snow was too wet and melted for us to leave tell-tale footprints. We squeezed into the gap.

"Don't make a noise," I warned Jason. "I mean it. If the Baxter brothers kill me, I'm gonna come back and kill you too."

Neil Baxter was the first to drop over the fence into the garden. He was the younger brother, the smaller one with the hoodie. He didn't see us. Then Matty Baxter climbed over. His eyes were narrow slits under his cap.

"Where'd they go?" Matty asked his younger brother.

Neil shrugged. "I didn't see. Maybe they know the person who lives here and they've gone in the house."

"Or just kept running, more like," Matty said.

I wanted to squeeze even further behind the shed but I didn't dare move. I was holding my breath.

A mobile phone started ringing. For a horrible second I thought it was mine. But the ring tone was different. It was Matty's. He took the phone out of his pocket and answered it.

"No, we lost him," he said into his phone. Then, "No idea. He was with his little brother but he got away!" He waited for the person on the other end of the phone to say something. "Yeah, OK, no worries," he said. At last he ended the call and put the phone back in his pocket.

"Johnny says not to hang around," Matty told his brother. "He says we can easily get him at school."

Neil grunted. "Less places to run and hide."

"He's always in the library anyway," Matty said. "That's where we'll get him."

They climbed back over the fence and into the alley.

When they'd gone, Jason shoved at me and we squeezed out of our hiding place.

"Wait," I told him. "Just hang on five minutes to make sure they've gone."

"I'm not waiting," he said. "I didn't even want to hide. You should have stood up to them."

"Yeah, right," I said. "Because that's what you would have done, is it? You'd have stood up to the Baxter brothers?"

Jason gave a shrug. He said, "I wouldn't have hidden from them."

I laughed at him. But I only half meant it. The problem was I reckoned Jason really would have stood up to them. He never backed down from anyone. He was always getting into fights. That was how he'd broken his arm. He'd fought a kid who'd picked on him because of his red hair. And this kid had been two years older than him.

"Let's just get to school," I said. But I didn't want to go back over the fence into the alley. We sneaked past the house and out onto the street in front. Then we went the long way across the playing fields. Just in case.

CHAPTER 4
Mrs Grace

As soon as we got close to the school it felt like everyone was looking at me. Jason ran off to meet a bunch of his mates. I had to walk up to the school alone. I knew other kids were staring at me. Heads turned to follow me.

I was sure they were whispering about me behind my back. Everyone knew Johnny Kemp was back. And everyone knew it was me who'd got him excluded.

I hated the stares and the whispers. I wanted to hide in the library. Miss Dean was in charge of the library. She was the school librarian and I was her head assistant. The library was closed today because Miss Dean didn't work on Mondays, but she'd trusted me with a set of keys and I was allowed to go there. But even the library didn't feel like it would be safe today, because the Baxter brothers knew they might find me there.

So I hung around near the entrance to the school, just in case I needed a quick escape. And I kept a look-out for Johnny Kemp and the Baxter brothers. I ignored everyone's stares as best as I could. I was also hoping I'd see Gary. But when the bell rang a few minutes later, I headed straight to my form room.

Gary was already sitting at his place – next to where I sat, at the back of the form room. There was a load of people around him. They all looked up when I walked in. Gary went red when he saw me. And I knew he was telling everyone his story about the Baxter brothers waiting for me. But maybe his story had a different ending. Maybe in his story he didn't really run away and leave me on my own.

Our form teacher, Mrs Grace, bustled into the room. "Sit down, sit down," she told everyone. "Quiet down, quiet down."

Everyone went to their seats. I sat down next to Gary.

"What happened?" he whispered. "You all right, yeah? Did Kemp get you?"

"No, he didn't get me," I whispered back. "But the Baxter brothers nearly did. And maybe if you hadn't run off, you could have helped."

I was glad to see Gary go red for a second time.

"And no talking!" Mrs Grace shouted. She was a big woman, sort of like an Easter egg on legs. She was always eating Polo mints and sometimes when she got angry she'd spit tiny bits of white mint out as she bellowed. She taught History and the walls of our form room were covered in pictures of battles and castles and soldiers from long ago.

Mrs Grace sat at her desk. She took the register and then she read out the day's notices.

She told us that on Saturday our school football team had lost 5–0 to Cooper Academy on the other side of town.

She warned us all for about the millionth time not to drop litter.

And then she said that there was going to be a trip to visit some museum somewhere …

But I didn't hear very much of anything Mrs Grace said. I was busy worrying about how I was going to keep out of Johnny Kemp's way, how I was going to survive. By the time the bell went for our first lesson, I knew that I needed help.

The rest of my form group, even Gary, all got out of the room quickly to head for their lessons. I went to talk to Mrs Grace. On her desk was a new packet of Polos and a stack of homework. She popped a mint in her mouth and started to mark the homework. She seemed to be using a lot of red pen.

She looked up at me before I'd had time to say a word. "Yes? What is it?" she asked.

I didn't really know how to say what I wanted to say. Was there a good or bad way to say it? So I just blurted it out.

"Johnny Kemp wants to beat me up."

Mrs Grace crunched on her Polo. "Johnny Kemp?"

"He's back at school today," I told her.

"I know he's back at school today," she said. "And he's beat you up, you say?"

I shook my head. "No. Not yet. But he wants to."

"He wants to beat you up?"

I nodded. "I was the one who got him kicked out."

"Yes, I know that," Mrs Grace said.

"He's told everyone he's going to kill me!" I was glad she was listening. Mrs Grace was one teacher even Johnny Kemp might not mess with.

"But has he beat you up yet?" she asked.

"No," I told her. Why did Mrs Grace keep repeating what I was saying?

Mrs Grace shrugged. "Well, there's nothing I can do about it then, is there?" She looked back at the homework in front of her and picked up her red pen again.

"What?" I was almost too shocked to say anything. "But ... but, Mrs Grace ..."

"You boys are worse than the girls most of the time," she said. " 'He did this, Mrs Grace. He said that, Mrs Grace!' I do hate all the moaning you boys do. Stand up for yourself. Be a man!" She spoke to me like I was stupid. "How can I blame Johnny Kemp for doing something he hasn't even done yet?"

And maybe I really was stupid – after all, I'd hoped she'd help me. "Can't you tell him not to beat me up?" I asked.

"Oh, I can tell him, yes," she said. "Do you think he'd listen?"

I looked down. "No."

"No," she agreed. "I don't either."

"But if he does beat me up …?" I asked.

Mrs Grace sighed as she took another Polo out of its packet. "If that happens, then yes. Come to me right away. The very moment he hits you, come to me and I'll do everything I can."

"Thank you, Mrs Grace," I said, but I didn't mean it.

"Now get to your first lesson," she told me as she popped the Polo in her mouth.

When I left the room I was even more worried and fed up than before.

As I went along to Maths I thought about what proof Mrs Grace would like so that she could see Johnny Kemp had hit me. Would a black eye be good enough? Or would she really like to see me with a broken arm? Maybe if he pulled one of my legs off I could hop back to her and ask her to help.

Mrs Grace had told me to stand up for myself. But I'd thought that by grassing on Johnny Kemp and getting him excluded, I'd been standing up for everyone else. I'd thought that getting Johnny Kemp kicked out was doing the whole school a favour.

First my mum and Gary, now Mrs Grace. The more people didn't want to listen to me, the angrier I felt.

CHAPTER 5
Neil Baxter

As soon as I walked into the Maths classroom I knew something was wrong. The room went totally silent. And every face looked at me.

Our teacher wasn't there yet. But Neil Baxter was. He wasn't in our Maths group but he was there, and he was sitting in my seat. He had his hood pulled up and he was scratching graffiti onto the table where I normally sat.

I didn't know what to do. I stood in the doorway and watched him. And everyone else in the class was watching me. Should I go up to him and tell him to get out of my chair? Should I ignore him and go and sit somewhere else?

I looked around the room. There was a free chair next to Ricky Hill. But when he saw me looking, he quickly put his bag on the chair to stop me from sitting there. Everyone was scared of Johnny Kemp and the Baxter brothers. No one wanted to get noticed by them.

I wished the teacher would hurry up, because he'd kick Neil Baxter out. But I couldn't stand there with everyone staring at me. I gripped my school bag tight. I told myself that if Neil Baxter ran at me now, I'd smack him with my bag as hard as I could.

"What d'you want?" I asked him.

The rest of the class turned from me to look at him. I could tell everyone in the room was holding their breath. They were waiting to see what was going to happen next.

Neil Baxter looked up at me. "I've got a message for you," he said. "From Johnny Kemp."

The whole class waited for him to tell me the message, but he didn't even open his mouth. He just kept scratching graffiti into the top of my table.

At last I had to ask, "So? What is this message?"

Again Neil Baxter looked at me. He pushed the chair back and stood up. He walked towards me. I gripped my bag even tighter. The whole class watched his every step. But he walked right past me and out of the classroom into the corridor.

I sighed. He'd gone, and that was something. My fingers had been gripping my bag so tightly that my hand hurt.

I went and sat down. Everyone in the room was talking now. The room was full of flying gossip. The words were like bullets and arrows, all aimed at me.

The Maths teacher strode into the room and hushed everyone. I looked at what Neil Baxter had scratched into the table.

DEAD MAN.

CHAPTER 6
Mr Powell

The first lesson of the day was over and I was still alive, but I was feeling more alone than ever.

Second lesson was P.E.

I kept my head down as I hurried along the corridor and tried to stay in the middle of the crowd. The gym block was on the other side of school. I walked the long way round to get to it, and I was checking my back all the way. I was ready to run the very second I saw Johnny Kemp.

He was nowhere. But I did see the Baxter brothers. They were waiting for me outside the entrance to the gym block. They stood there like bouncers guarding the doors. They probably wanted to bounce me all the way to Johnny Kemp. I was going to have to walk past them to get inside. Just then I spotted Mr Powell having a hard time as he tried to carry five footballs all at once. He almost had to juggle them to stop them from falling to the ground. I scurried over to him.

"Can I help you with them, sir?" I asked.

He gave me two of the footballs. "Good lad, Dan. Top man. Thank you."

Both Neil and Matty scowled at me as I walked in between them and into the gym block.

"Shouldn't you two be in a lesson somewhere?" Mr Powell asked them. "Get those creaky brains working, eh?"

They nodded at Mr Powell, but snarled at me as they slunk away. I grinned at them – I'd escaped that time. They didn't dare do anything to me with Mr Powell there. And that gave me another idea.

I followed Mr Powell into the P.E. store down at the end of the gym block. "Just put the balls in the box by the door," he said.

The store room was full of football nets, cricket bats, hockey sticks and hurdles for athletics. It was cramped and muddy and smelly. I put the footballs away.

"Er, Mr Powell? Can I have a quick word?" I asked.

"As long as it's quick," he told me. "The lesson should've started two minutes ago."

Mr Powell was a tall man with a shiny bald head. He always wore a green tracksuit and chunky trainers. He always had a whistle hanging on a string around his neck, too. Most of the kids at school liked him because he wasn't that old and could be a good laugh. And he liked the kids who were good at football or basketball. My best sport was badminton, so I never knew if he liked me or not. Johnny Kemp had been in the school football team. Did Mr Powell like him? I guessed Kemp might like Mr Powell. And so I reckoned that if anyone could get Kemp to leave me alone, it was going to be Mr Powell.

"Did you know Johnny Kemp is back at school today?" I asked, trying to make it sound like no big deal.

Mr Powell nodded. "Yes. Yes, I did!" He grinned. "And if you're about to tell me you're sorry about what happened, then don't worry, Dan. It's OK. All is forgiven, lad."

I didn't have a clue what he meant.

"Thank goodness he's back, eh?" Mr Powell went on, his grin getting bigger. "I'll tell you something for nothing. We need him back, that's for sure."

I didn't understand. "You're happy he's back?" I asked.

"That's right. Totally. 110% happy," Mr Powell said. "Did you hear how badly the school football team got beaten on Saturday? 5–0. Good God. 5–0. And by that bunch of buffoons at Cooper Academy too!" He tutted and shook his head. "Johnny Kemp is our star player. I tried to tell the Head that he should let Johnny play even if he was excluded, but would that man listen to me? Would he?" Mr Powell shook his head and tutted again.

"But, sir ...!" I tried.

"Now I know it was all your doing that Johnny got excluded," Mr Powell said. "And I suppose by rights I should be blaming you for our shocking, shocking defeat. But, well, I guess you thought you were doing the right thing!" He patted my head like I was a dog. "Let's leave it at that, eh?"

"But he says he's going to beat me up, sir. He's told me he'll kill me. He's told everyone he will."

Mr Powell's smile fell away. "What did you say?"

"Johnny Kemp," I said. "He says he's going to kill me. Because I was the one who got him excluded."

Mr Powell looked hard at me. He gritted his teeth and pointed a long finger at me. "Now just you listen here. Don't you go spreading any more rumours and bad feelings!" He leaned in towards me. His whistle swung on its string around his neck. "Are you listening? Do you hear me? Our football team needs Johnny Kemp. It's for the good of the school."

I took a step backwards before he could prod me in the chest. "What about the good of me?" I mumbled.

Mr Powell narrowed his eyes at me. The overhead light glinted off his bald head. "I didn't say anything to you before, but I'm telling you right now. The worst thing in the world is a snitch. The kind of person I really, really can't stand is a grass and a snitch. Do you understand what I'm saying? No one respects that kind of person."

I was stunned, gobsmacked. First my mum, then Gary and Mrs Grace. Now Mr Powell too. No one wanted to help me.

Mr Powell stood up straight and puffed out his chest. "Go and get changed," he told me. "The rest of the class will be playing basketball in the gym today, but I think you could do with some fresh air out on the field. I think it will clear your mind, help you think about what I've said. I want 20 laps of the running track before break."

CHAPTER 7
Gary

By break time I had still only run 15 laps of the track, so Mr Powell wouldn't let me stop. He stood on the field wearing a fleece over his tracksuit top, drinking a steaming mug of tea, and he made sure I ran the full 20. I left a mushy grey circuit of footprints in the snow.

'Look on the bright side,' I thought. 'At least no one can beat me up while I'm doing this.'

I'd been worried about where I was going to hide during break. But running round and round the track made it impossible for Johnny Kemp or the Baxter brothers to get close.

At last, when I'd huffed and puffed my way around 20 laps, Mr Powell let me stop and get changed again.

"Good lad," he said. "Now you just remember what I've told you."

I dragged my worn-out legs to my R.E. lesson.

And I was thinking that maybe Mr Powell was right. Maybe I had broken some kind of secret rule by grassing up Johnny Kemp. I'd thought people would be happy having the biggest bully and thug the school had ever seen excluded. I thought the school had been a calmer, more friendly place without him. Gary and I had talked about it. Gary had said he was glad Kemp was gone.

But now Johnny Kemp was back and no one wanted anything to do with me any more.

I was getting used to the whispers and stares by this time, so I ignored the way everyone looked at me when I walked into R.E. I plonked myself down at my desk and listened to Mr Stokes drone on about "Forgiveness". I nearly put my hand up to tell him it was Johnny Kemp he should be talking to, not us.

Halfway through the lesson, a scrunched-up ball of paper landed on my desk. I turned around to see who had thrown it at me, but no one was looking my way. When I looked closer I saw there was writing on the paper. Carefully I pulled the crumpled paper open and flattened it out. I didn't know whose writing it was on it.

The note said –

"Johnny Kemp's going to get you at lunch time."

As I was reading it, a second ball of paper landed in front of me. Again I looked for who had thrown it, but no one was looking my way.

This 2nd note read –

"There's nowhere to hide. He'll find you."

When a 3rd crumpled-up note was thrown at me I didn't even bother to read it. I brushed it off my desk and onto the floor. A 4th and 5th one flew towards me and I did the same with them. Someone just wanted to wind me up and scare me. And I didn't want them to know it was working.

At last the bell rang for the end of the lesson and everyone jumped up to leave. Should I try talking to Mr Stokes? I reckoned it would be a waste of time. What with all of that "Forgiveness" stuff he was going on about, he'd probably want Kemp to kill me just so I could go on to forgive him in the after-life. I followed everyone out into the corridor.

And a hand grabbed my shoulder …

I ran.

Didn't even look back. Just charged off down the corridor.

Heart thumping. Legs pumping. Pushing people out of my way.

Until Gary's voice shouted, "Dan. Dan! It's me."

I stopped and turned around. My heart was thumping so hard it was making the whole of my body shake.

"Sorry," Gary said. "Didn't mean to brick you up."

"I thought you were Johnny Kemp," I said.

"Sorry," he said again. Then he whispered, "Listen, I need to talk to you!" He grabbed my sleeve and pulled me towards the boys' toilets. "Come on. In here."

I followed him into the toilets. The first thing Gary did was check the cubicles. He shoved the doors open one at a time, to make sure no one was there. He didn't want anyone else to hear what he was going to say. What could be so important, so secret? I reckoned it must have something to do with Johnny Kemp.

Gary was a little bit taller than me, but I always beat him at arm wrestling. He never answered teachers back. He always handed his homework in on time. He was pale and skinny and sometimes he looked like he was worried his own shadow might punch him. He had always had it rough when Johnny Kemp was around. He was such an easy target for bullies.

I also knew he wasn't the sort of person to skip lessons. If he was hiding in the toilets with me instead of going to Geography, then something really serious must have happened.

Gary paced up and down in front of the row of sinks underneath the long mirror. "I've got to talk to you about Johnny Kemp," he said.

"Why?" I asked. "Who says?"

"The Baxter brothers. They got me at break!"
He pulled up the sleeve of his jumper to show me
a nasty red mark on his arm where either Neil or
Matty had given him a Chinese burn.

"Ouch," I said. "Looks like that really hurts."

"Not as bad as this!" Gary lifted up his
jumper to show me his chest. He had bruises
around both nipples where the brothers had
given them a spiteful twisting. "And they
said they're going to do worse unless you give
yourself up!" He turned around to look in the
mirror and made a face.

"Give myself up?" I asked.

Gary turned back to face me and pulled his
jumper down again. "That's what they said. At
lunch, yeah? You've got to meet Kemp round the
back of the science block."

I shook my head. "No way. I can't. He's not
just going to hurt me. He's going to kill me. You
know that."

"Listen," Gary said. "They said they were
only starting with me. They reckon they're not
going to chase you any more –"

"Like hell."

"That's what they told me," Gary went on. "They've given up chasing you. But you've got to go to them."

I shook my head again. "No way. There's no way I'm going to do that."

"You have to," Gary insisted. "They said that from now on, every break and lunch time, Kemp is going to beat up a different kid. I was the first, and they said I got it easy because they wanted me to pass on the message. They're going to get a different kid this lunch time who's going to have it ten times worse than me!" I could tell by the look in his eyes that he wasn't joking. "And then another tomorrow break, and another tomorrow lunch time. Different kids getting done over every day until you give yourself up."

It was hard to believe it. But Gary was nodding his head, his face dead serious.

"You have to meet him," he told me. "You have to."

"Would you?" I asked.

Gary looked puzzled.

"Come on," I said. "If you were me, would you meet him?"

"But it's not me," Gary said. "I'm not the one who grassed him up and got him kicked out."

"And you know why I grassed him up, don't you?" I asked. "I did it because of people like you."

Gary was going to argue with me.

I didn't let him. "Over these last two weeks, yeah?" I asked. "These two weeks when Kemp's not been around? How many times have you had your lunch money stolen from you?"

Gary stared at his feet. "None," he said.

"Exactly. And Kemp used to steal it off you at least twice a week before that, didn't he? You and loads of other kids!" I couldn't help feeling angry. "I did you all a favour by grassing him up and getting him excluded. But no one's helped me out today. Everyone's just stared at me like I was a freak, or they've ignored me. Why should I care if Johnny Kemp goes round beating you all up?"

Gary didn't know how to answer that. The way he looked at me, it was like I was the one who'd given him Chinese burns and nipple twists. "But what am I going to say to the Baxter brothers?" he asked.

"Tell them to piss off."

Gary looked like he might burst into tears. And I felt sorry for him. But I really hated myself for feeling sorry for him. I shook my head, angry at myself and at the rest of the world around me.

But maybe I had a plan too.

"OK," I said. "Tell them this. Tell them that I'm going to be in the library at lunch time. And the only way I'm going to meet Kemp round the back of the science block is if they drag me there themselves."

Gary still didn't look happy.

"That's it," I told him. "That's my message!"

Then I left him in the toilets. But I didn't go to my Geography lesson. I went straight to the library.

CHAPTER 8
Baxter Brothers

I had my library keys, so I let myself in. The library was a long, thin room with a high ceiling. All the bookshelves were around the edge, with computers on tables in the middle. It was one of the biggest rooms in the school. It could get noisy at lunch times, but right now it felt calm and peaceful with no one else there. Very peaceful. It felt great to be on my own and not have other kids staring or whispering, and not have to be checking that no one was after me. I liked books and I liked computers and I liked being in the library.

I checked the shelves that were in the corner of the room. They were broken, and Miss Dean had asked for them to be mended a few weeks ago. I could see the caretaker still hadn't mended them. Miss Dean thought they were dangerous. The whole bookcase could pull away from the wall and fall over without warning. I knew she wouldn't be happy that it hadn't been fixed over the weekend. On Friday she had taken all the books down from those shelves and stacked them on the floor. I put the books back. Not in any proper order.

I just made sure the heaviest books were at the top.

Then I sat by one of the computers and waited for lunch time, waited for the Baxter brothers.

The bell for lunch rang at 1:00 p.m.

Neil and Matty Baxter walked into the library at 1:02 p.m.

I was still sitting at the computer, but I got up quickly. I had a plan. But it wasn't much of a plan. Now I felt it was probably the worst plan in the world.

Matty Baxter looked at me from underneath the peak of his cap. "Johnny Kemp wants to see you. Now."

"He knows where I am," I said. I wanted to sound braver than I felt. "Tell him to come here."

Matty looked at his brother. Then back at me. "You're just making it worse for yourself," he said. "Do you want us to do to you what we did to your friend Gary?"

"I'm not going anywhere," I said.

The brothers looked at each other. Neil gave a shrug. Matty nodded. Then all of a sudden they both ran at me.

They were wanting to trap me like they'd tried to do in the alley before school. But this time it was my trap.

Neil came around the island of computer tables one way, and Matty came the other. I jumped up onto the tables and ran along them from one end of the library to the other.

I jumped down and ran to the broken shelves. Neil was quicker than his brother. He was the first to come running at me. But I was even quicker. I grabbed the biggest book I could and smacked him round the head with it.

Neil grunted and his eyes scrunched up in surprised pain.

I swung the book at him again. It made a heavy thudding sound as it bounced off the side of his skull. He staggered backwards, holding his head in both hands. I barged into the tall shelves and slammed them with all my weight. And the whole bookcase wobbled, then tipped, then fell. All those massive books came tumbling out as the shelves pitched forward. Neil yelped as the books hit him. But the bookcase itself was even heavier.

Neil tried to hold it up. "Grab it," he shouted at me.

But I ignored him. He couldn't keep the bookcase from falling. He just wasn't strong enough to hold it up any more. It collapsed on top of him. He was trapped underneath.

I ran.

But now Matty was in front of me. And I didn't have a plan to stop this brother.

Matty made a grab for me. I dived underneath the computer tables this time. I scurried on my hands and knees along the floor, in and out of the thick computer cables.

I could see Matty's legs at the end of the tables. He was blocking my way out. I couldn't escape. He was swearing at me, calling me every name he could think of. Dangling down by my head was a 3-pin plug on the end of a cable. I grabbed it. And as hard as I could, I stabbed it down into the top of Matty's trainer.

He howled. I mashed the plug through the thin canvas of his trainer and into the top of his foot. He leaped away, screaming.

I took my chance and shot out from under the table and ran for the door. Neil was trying to squirm out from underneath the collapsed shelf. Matty was on the floor clutching his foot. I ducked out into the corridor and slammed the door shut behind me. Then I got out my keys again. I locked the Baxter brothers inside.

Now I just had to deal with Johnny Kemp.

CHAPTER 9
Johnny Kemp

The news was out. Johnny was going to get me. There were maybe a hundred kids round the back of the science block waiting to see me get killed.

The science block was well away from the staff room. No teachers would see. This was where the smokers came for a quick fag. There was a greenhouse and a messy pond for outdoor Biology lessons. The plants in the greenhouse looked dead and the pond was murky, with a thin skin of ice on top.

I had to push through the crowd of kids to get to the patch of grass next to the pond. I could hear whispers and mutters everywhere. The kids shoved and pushed to get a better look at me. They all knew who I was – I'd got Johnny Kemp kicked out in the first place. Now I was going to be really famous for getting myself kicked in.

It didn't feel good. I didn't want to be the most famous dead kid in school.

My mouth was dry. My heart was beating fast. This had been my plan. Get rid of the Baxter brothers and meet Johnny Kemp face to face, one on one. I was hoping I could talk him out of wanting to kill me. I thought maybe when the Baxter brother bodyguards weren't around that I could talk to him, reason with him. I'd known all along it wasn't much of a plan. Now that I was here, it felt like the worst plan in the world ever.

I decided I wasn't going to make it easy for him. I wasn't just going to give up. If he was going to kill me, he was going to have to fight me first.

The crowd of kids fell silent and then parted like curtains at the front of a stage. Johnny Kemp came through the middle of them. He stood opposite me.

He was a year older than me and almost a head taller. He had very short dark hair and eyes like hard black pebbles. He didn't look big and beefy – he looked like thickly twisted wire. He had a red scar on his cheek. If you believed the stories, he'd got that scar when he was bitten by a pit bull. And people said that Kemp had bitten the dog back.

Johnny Kemp was in front of me. He was less than a metre away from me. His breath steamed from his lips like he was on fire inside. His hard eyes locked onto me.

I wanted to meet his eyes, stare back at him, but I couldn't. My eyes danced here, there and everywhere. I could feel my legs tremble and I hoped he didn't notice.

I looked at the crowd of kids all around. They'd all moved closer, all wanting to see.

I scanned their faces. I knew who they all were, but I knew none of them were going to help me.

"Listen," I said to Johnny Kemp. I tried to smile. "We don't have to fi –"

But he jumped at me, pushed at me. He hit me in the chest like a battering ram and knocked me backwards. I slipped on the wet, slushy grass and went down. I scrambled to get my feet underneath me again, tried to get back up, but he was too quick for me. He lifted his fist. He stood over me. I bucked and thrashed underneath him. Somehow I pushed him over and stood up again at last.

He was the one on the ground on his back now. And I knew I could kick him. I could lift my foot up and then plant it hard in his stomach or his face. But I didn't.

I waited until he had stood up again. Then I kicked him in the balls.

He howled. The crowd all went, "Ooooh."

I was hoping that kick would stop him in his tracks, but he must have had balls harder than coconuts because all too quickly he jumped at me again. And this time, when he knocked me to the ground he made sure he kept me there. He was on top of me, pinning me down on my back.

I saw his fist go up. But it was too quick for me to see on the way down. He hit me once. Twice. All sorts of fireworks went off behind my eyes. I felt sick and dizzy with pain. He hit me again.

I tried hard to push him off. I reached out towards the crowd. Would someone – anyone – grab my hand and pull me out from underneath him? No. No one did.

So he hit me again. And again.

When he lifted his fist one more time I could see blood. My blood. I just wanted it all to be over now. At least if he really did kill me it wouldn't hurt as bad as this. And nothing could hurt as bad as I'd been feeling all morning. Being as lonely as that hurt more than anything in the world.

From somewhere I found one more bit of strength, one more muscle that I didn't even know I had. With a grunt and a heave I managed to push Johnny Kemp off and roll out from under him. It must have given him a shock. He'd thought he'd won. He was off-balance and he fell backwards.

I saw I'd surprised him. I also saw the pond behind him. I shoved at him with a grunt. He sprawled backwards. He tried to turn to catch himself, put his hands out to save himself, but he smashed right through the thin ice and into the freezing, dirty water. I jumped at him.

I was on his back. I pushed his face down into the water. Now I was winning.

Johnny Kemp tried to grab at something. His hands couldn't get a grip on the pond's slippery sides. I kept his face down under the water. He was like a snake underneath me, but I held on. He bucked and twisted, the water bubbled and churned, but I wouldn't let him go.

The crowd of kids was silent now. I could hear that silence louder than when they'd been shouting. I could feel all their eyes on me. I wrapped my fingers in Johnny Kemp's hair and jerked his head up out of the water.

"Leave me alone," I shouted. "Say it! Say you'll leave me alone."

Kemp hissed at me, still full of venom and spite.

So I shoved him under the water again. His finger nails scraped the icy sides of the pond but he still couldn't get a grip.

I yanked his head up again, ripping out a big clump of his hair.

"I mean it. Leave me alone!" I shouted.

The venom was leaking out of him. I could see it in his eyes. He didn't care about me any more, he just didn't want to be pushed back under the water again. I reckoned that maybe he was about ready to give up.

But I pushed him under the water again.

I knew the other kids were seeing me win and I liked it. I was winning a fight against Johnny Kemp. I was doing the hurting instead of being hurt. I could feel my blood fizzing around my body. And I knew how easy it would be to keep him under the water. He wasn't fighting so hard any more. He was weak and worn out.

I knew that if I wanted to, I could keep his head under the water for ever.

But at last I let him up, let him go. He crawled to one side on his hands and knees, coughing and choking. He fell on his side, gasping for breath.

I stood up carefully. I hurt all over from the fight. I wiped at my bloody nose. I said, "I beat you. Everyone saw me beat you."

Johnny Kemp didn't say anything. He vomited up a puddle of brown water.

And that's when the crowd of kids burst into cheers and shouts. I was shocked at first. They ran forward to tell me how great I was, how amazing the fight had been.

But were they really cheering me? I was shocked, and then angry. I knew that I hated them. All of them. They would have cheered Johnny Kemp even louder if he'd won.

So I pushed them away from me, pushed my way past them. I ignored them all. Everyone except Gary.

He came bouncing over to me, all smiles. "That was brilliant, Dan," he said. "You were brilliant."

"So now I'm everyone's friend again?" I asked.

Gary looked puzzled.

I was so angry I was scared I might explode.

"So everyone ignores me," I said. "No one wants to help me, but now I've beaten Johnny Kemp they all want to be my friend?"

Gary tried to smile again, but he looked worried.

I held out my hand. "Give me your lunch money," I told him.

He took a step away from me. "What?"

"You heard," I said. "Give me your lunch money."

He shook his head. "Dan, what's ...? You're joking, right?"

"I've never been more serious in my life," I said. I looked at the old bully still on the ground by the pond. There were kids all around him. They weren't scared of him any more. Then I looked back at Gary.

"I'm the new Johnny Kemp," I told him. "Give me every penny you've got."

Our books are tested
for children and young people by
children and young people.

Thanks to everyone who consulted on
a manuscript for their time and effort in
helping us to make our books better
for our readers.

*Also by **Keith Gray** ...*

Toby is a murderer.

That's what the ghost at the end of his
bed tells him.

But Toby's just a boy who loves comics,
and gets called a geek by his big brother.
He'd never kill anyone ...

Or would he?

Four people. Four stories.
Four links in the chain.

Cal is sick of being the good guy. Joe's
dad is a big-time loser. Ben has two
girlfriends but only loves himself. Kate
has to say the hardest goodbye of all.

One book, which will change their lives
forever ...

www.barringtonstoke.co.uk